Feral Within © 2024, Elreydelleon Fox

ISBN: 978-1-7348255-8-9

This novel is entirely fantastical. Though there is reference to real-life locales, the characters within experience fictitious events. Let your imagination see the world through each character's eyes. View this adventure from your own unique perspective, for that's where the real heart of the story settles.

Feral Within

By E. Fox

Chapter 1

This was one of the coldest nights of my life.

The hard ground was unforgiving, and to be thrown out a mere couple nights after Christmas made it even more unbearable. All because of a misunderstanding, and no way to rectify the matter overnight. She simply wouldn't have it.

"You said we could splurge for the holidays, Leon, and look where that put us!"

"No, I said we could *after* the holidays." My words were very direct.

"That's how you always explain it. You say one thing, and then claim it was something different."

"And you never listen to what I say the first time!"

Of course, this was the wrong thing to say at the wrong time. She said I could return in a couple of days, which meant I was roughing it the next night as well.

My girlfriend and I moved here last month. We've been acclimating well enough, but unfortunately a number of other problems have arisen, and it always seems to revolve around money. Personally, I'm not too worried about this, but my lack of concern is a major problem for her.

Sure, I'm no minimalist, but I think there are a lot of things we could do without. Living in the lap of luxury is only afforded by those who already have enough put away, not after moving.

Honestly, I wish I could move further south where it's warmer, but we'll have to start saving again before that's even a remote possibility. At least this year has been kinder, as far as the weather is concerned.

No snow had fallen yet, much to my surprise, as it's typical to expect a few feet by this time of year in Maine. Despite this, the air was still very frigid out here in the woods.

I made do with what little I had. I managed to stuff my duffel with a blanket, and had a nice jacket over my sweater. Amidst all of my belongings, I'd forgotten to remove a bag of leftovers, and now I'm thankful for that.

Apparently, I also forgot to grab my phone before I was rushed out the door. At least I had a watch on. A cheap, but durable one at that. My girlfriend got me a nicer one for Christmas, suggesting that it'd make me look more professional, but I like this one because it glows in the dark.

It was after midnight. I had to travel a little far to find solace. Not that I would've turned down the opportunity to stay in town, but since we moved here only a month ago, I didn't know anyone else. The bars were closed for the holiday season, and shelter space scarce as could be, more so in the winter. Besides, I didn't want to be awoken after just a few hours of shoddy sleep.

I've never had what one would call a normal schedule. "Early to bed, early to rise" did not become me, and I found life a lot easier to manage once I had graduated years ago. No, the night life suited me well, and I found it enjoyable to have ample quiet time to myself. Nevertheless, this… this was a little more than I bargained for. Never before have I walked so far, so late into the night.

Worn out from my unprecedented hike, I settle down into the unfamiliar forest, taking refuge under the starlit canopy. I found a nook in which to try and keep warm between a couple of large, red oaks. Beyond the evergreens in barren patches the sky was very much illuminated, apart from some clouds passing through. Even more brilliant was the moon, as its face shone upon everything beneath.

There's no wind tonight, thankfully, but the lack of a chilly breeze made every other little sound noticeable. A few times I heard the shuffling of foliage from passing creatures, though I never saw any. A short while later, I started to hear howling.

Wolves, no doubt. Probably a pack singing to the night.

The chorus went on for what felt like an hour, and then stopped. I have no idea how long wolves keep up a song, but even I thought it strange to suddenly hear nothing.

Without warning, I heard a single howl a lot closer. A loud, guttural voice piercing the air, and I knew that I would not be sleeping tonight.

I sat up, watching for any sign of movement, but didn't see anything. The darkness surrounding me felt very thick all of a sudden, as if someone put the forest into an airtight container.

My breath shortened, and I was hesitant to breathe at all. Once again, the howl sounded, closer still. Glancing around, there was nothing out of the ordinary, until I saw it.

A shaded silhouette against the pitch of night stared directly at me, two small, yellow lights not more than a dozen yards off, looking straight into my eyes.

Frozen in place by fear more than cold, I tried to move my numb legs. Eventually, my body conceded to thought, taking off in a sprint.

Satchel at my side, I ran through the trees, trying not to trip over any obstacles. My chest burned from the sudden intake of cold air, but I figured I'd feel a lot worse in a matter of seconds if I stopped.

My nerves steeled me to keep running for a few minutes, blood pounding in my ears, before I finally collapsed, gasping hard. I shot around again, but didn't see anything, and dropped my head in exhaustion.

As my heart began to slow, I looked up, only to see those lights staring back, now only several feet in front of me. There was no way I was going to outrun whatever this was, as it managed to circle around without my noticing.

I sat, slowly shuffling backward as it approached me, seemingly quadruped. The lights were attached to a set of eyes, golden orbs illuminated by the open branches above, two pupils blazing all the brighter as the eyeshine reflected back at me.

It was a big wolf. A *very* big wolf.

Standing at around four feet, the animal stepped ever closer, looking down at me as I stared up into its eyes. I didn't want to come off as provocative, but I could not tear my gaze away out of a strange mixture between trepidation and curiosity.

The wolf did not growl, nor did it even bear its teeth.

"What... what do you want with me? I'm not out here to hunt, so I don't want to hurt you... but I—"

Not a fraction of a second later, I found myself against the dirt, pressed beneath the sheer weight of its legs as claws dug into clothing, sharp teeth against my neck.

I ran cold, almost totally numb as I felt blood drain, vision growing dark. Struggling for a short time, I knew I couldn't possibly overthrow the wolf's strength, and so gave up. I lay there, certain I was dead on the spot. I was going to die out here on the cold, hard earth, and there was not a thing I could do about it.

After a few short moments, the huge wolf sat back, leaving behind a large amount of saliva. If I didn't know any better, I'd have laughed at how repulsive it was to be covered in slime while I lay here dying, but... I never did pass out.

Breathing labored, I lay there sprawled across the ground while an unusual tingling sensation drifted from my neck through my body, as though life were returning in a trickle.

A few tears left my eyes when I realized that I wasn't going to die, while the wolf sat stolidly, licking blood from its fur.

Chapter 2

"You..."

It looks at me briefly, before returning to clean.

"You didn't kill me," I continue, entirely staggered.

"And you didn't kill me."

My nerves tingle again, only this time in astonishment. *Did this wolf really just talk to me?*

I didn't notice any movement from its lips, but I swear I heard the muddled voice of a female.

Slowly easing up onto an arm, I speak again. "Did you just say something?"

The wolf looks back up at me, staring hard as lips indeed move. "It'd be rude not to."

Shuddering, I find no more words to offer. This wolf was definitely talking, and she didn't try to hide it.

"Why do you fear me? You said you weren't out here to hunt, so I found no reason to kill you."

"That—that's true, but you bit me."

"I was hungry. You left me with little choice." Her tongue slides between a paw. "Besides, killing prey only makes it that much more difficult to sustain a source of feeding."

"How come you went for me, instead of an elk or something?"

She sets her paw down and rises on two legs, towering far above me. Around seven feet of furred muscle looms on digitigrade legs, hard eyes scanning me intently. "Game is hard to find this time of year, especially with other wolf packs around, so I settle for wandering idiots like yourself. Humans are much easier to feed off."

My brows furrow. "Um, don't vampires do that?"

She spits in disgust—an odd-looking behavior for a wolf—before shouting. "Don't you *dare* compare me to such a vile creature!"

Taken aback, I shut my eyes, nearly deafened.

I hear a huff. "Besides, vampires don't exist. Everyone knows that." She shuffles a bit, before speaking again. "Stop cowering like prey!"

Eyes open, I decide it better to stand, getting up, and almost stumble as I find my footing. "What are you?"

Surprisingly, a faint grin appears. "I'm a werewolf, of course."

So, vampires don't exist, but werewolves do. If I'm not dead, I'm obviously dreaming.

Running a hand against my neck, I see that there's not much of a wound to be found. Only a slick remnant over a shallow gash.

The werewolf comments on my discovery. "Our saliva… it's very potent stuff. We don't lick at our wounds for the sake of beauty."

"Okay, so I'm apparently ignorant to your kind in general. Correct me if I'm wrong, but don't I have anything else to worry about?"

"Not unless you hate werewolves."

Her statement didn't come off as antipathy, but rather more like concern.

She speaks again. "Maybe a more formal introduction. Why don't you go first?"

I consider her inquiry momentarily. "I'm Leon."

"A strong name. Mine is Waya."

"That seems a bit unique."

"It was given to me many years ago. I… don't remember my original name." Her eyes stare off to the side.

Original name?

Before I can ask, Waya begins to wander off, looking back briefly. "I hope you don't intend on going into the local town for a day. It's not safe." She drops to all fours and sets out, gone beyond the dark trees in a matter of seconds.

I sit in the twilight of morning, a weak fire pitifully flaring against the dark slate of the sky, dull grey breaching the treetops.

After the event a few hours ago, I thought I'd be completely exhausted. Instead, I only feel moderately tired, but totally alert. Adrenaline can do strange things to you.

A slight pain in my chest subsided about an hour ago. It felt weird, to say the least. I had no trouble breathing, but couldn't get up. When I finally managed, I collected any loose tinder and wood to be seen, firing it up with a couple matches I found on my way out of town.

Shuddering against the cold, I eventually concede in trying to sleep before the sun can rise. To my amazement, it didn't take long at all.

Eyes opening with a start, a surreal night encapsulates me as I fly through the trees, suspended a fair bit off the ground. I love flying dreams, and even though I can faintly feel my feet below me, I don't bother looking down.

Taking off into the darkness, my eyes adjust easily, and find no trouble navigating.

I slow down, suddenly aware of the faint scent of warmth, exciting me in the bare cold of winter. Unable to help myself, I pick up speed toward the sensation.

The next instant, I'm pressed to the ground, face nuzzled into a warm blanket. It's as though I'm enjoying a bowl of hot soup as my mind settles, completely content with a satisfied appetite.

The call of a raven startles me, morning haze greeting my eyes on a heavily overcast setting.

I'm curled up on the ground, feeling no real hunger from the dream. Maybe I just have no appetite after what I witnessed last night.

Then again, perhaps it was a double dream, and nothing happened at all. That's what I'd have believed anyway, until I saw the condition of my clothing.

My shirt, sweater and pants were fairly loose, showing signs of tearing, and my jacket and belt were practically destroyed. For some reason, I can't really recall what happened with Waya, but I guess she must have roughed me up pretty bad. I was likely far more tired than I remember being, and wasn't aware of the shredding. What's terrible is that the front of my sweater was also covered in blood. That bite I suffered must've been worse than I thought.

Just when it couldn't get any worse, it does. Stretching my back with a twist, a horrifying sight catches my attention, sending a shout from me.

Laying behind me was a deer carcass, a large portion missing from the middle. I freak out, getting away from it.

Waya probably left it for me, thinking I'd make use of the meat, but I'm even less hungry now.

What kind of sick joke is this supposed to be?

I check my watch and gape. Apparently, an extra day had passed while I slept. My body likely needed the time to recover from loss of blood.

Getting up, I try to set my belt again, but to no avail. Frustrated, I removed the drawstring from my sweater and fixed it through the belt loops. Thinking about possible reactions from townsfolk, I turned my sweater inside-out.

I approach the town cautiously. It's a Friday, busy and cold enough to keep most people working indoors. Seeing that the coast is clear, I make my way back to our apartment.

When I step inside, my girlfriend comes through the living room. "Leon, what the heck happened?! Did you get in a fight?"

"What do you mean?"

"Your face… half of it's covered in blood!"

I run into the bathroom, and glance in the mirror. The bottom-half of my face is stained with crimson, as are my teeth.

She steps in behind me, deep concern drawn upon her face. "I'm sorry I tossed you out. I didn't mean for this to happen to you."

"It's… it's okay."

With a scoff, my girlfriend retrieves a washcloth, soaking it thoroughly for me. "There we are. You should probably shave, too, because you look like a bum," she says with a giggle.

I look back up at the mirror as I clean my face, seeing quite a bit of color covering my skin. My facial hair doesn't grow quickly, but then, I didn't take the time to examine it before I had to leave. Having dark hair makes it more noticeable, too. "Yeah, I'll do that before I go to bed."

We sit for a quiet dinner that night. She made meatloaf, one of my favorite dishes, but despite my time being gone, I still don't feel like eating.

"What's the matter, honey? It's your favorite!"

"I'm just not feeling very hungry, that's all."

She sighs. "Look, I already said I'm sorry. Can you please try to eat something before bed?"

Reluctantly, I force myself to eat my portion. It tastes terribly bland and lacking, but then, she never really was the best cook. Of course, I wouldn't ever say that to her face.

Bed time has come for me, and I settle in after brushing my teeth and shaving my face clean, sliding beneath warm covers after a quiet night of doing nothing. I embrace my girlfriend, arms holding her close to me, and find peaceful rest, leaving behind the worries of my trek in the forest.

Chapter 3

The next day, I get up to a quiet apartment, feeling exceptionally rested.

I wander out to the kitchenette, and see a note sitting upon the counter.

Morning lovebug,

I left you some bacon and eggs in the microwave. One of my coworkers said she wanted to hang out after work for a bit today, so I'll probably be home in the evening. Please try to complete that job application so you can turn it in on Monday. I'm sure you'd be a good fit.

After devouring the breakfast, I proceed to fill out the papers, making good on my efforts to work toward sustaining our new living space. Washing dishes isn't my idea of a fun time, but at least it's easy.

It was a very dull couple of hours afterward, wasting the afternoon away on the computer.

Curiosity gets the best of me, and soon my browsing becomes more focused. I cannot help but to punch in my inquiry, results returning instantly. My eyes scan the pages as a couple of notes stand out to me.

"Werewolves, also know as lycanthropes, are individuals found within folklore. A hybrid of therianthropy between a human and wolf, a werewolf is often detailed to be seen on nights with a full moon.

"Dating back to the medieval era, it was often believed that such transformations fell under the application of witchcraft, causing an uproar in local steads. Many supposed creatures were hunted down to purge the lands of such evil practices, yet no proof of these beings was ever found, despite numerous reported sightings."

I sit back, discontented with my short-lived research effort. Even though I doubt my own experience, there's just too much of a remnant to back it up. I consider for a moment whether or not reporting to the authorities, but ultimately decide otherwise.

My girlfriend returns as expected with the setting sun. "I'm home! If you're not doing anything, we can get some shopping done before it gets any colder tonight."

"Sure, I guess we can do that."

She stares at me.

"What?"

"I thought you said you were going to shave before bed."

"I did!"

She gives me an incredulous look. "No, you clearly didn't."

I head into the bathroom, and see my face just as it was last night. "What the…?"

"You were probably just imagining it," she yells from the living room.

It's true that I get tired enough some nights to imagine my actions, but I'm certain this was no delusion. Of course, that wouldn't be saying much in light of recent events if it were.

With another shaving job complete, we head out.

The walk wasn't very far. Ten minutes later, we're navigating a couple of aisles, picking out goods for the week.

We stop in the meat section, looking at the deal on steaks.

I pick up a pack of two. "What do you think of this?"

"Hmm, looks alright." She sets it into the basket.

Someone standing near to us turns around. "Leon? Is that you?" She's in a long, black dress, with gloves to match. Her face is wrapped in a thick niqab, shadowed yellowish-brown eyes peering from within.

"Do I know you?"

"It's me, Waya!"

My girlfriend scoffs. "We just moved here. You don't know him."

This girl doesn't sound entirely like Waya, but those eyes are awfully interesting, being such an unusual color. It's difficult to ascertain with her head concealed, but she looks like a normal human to me.

"I'm sorry… I don't recognize you."

"I don't doubt that. It was pretty late at night."

I hear the basket drop. "So that's what you did with your time away? Guess that explains the faint mark on your neck."

"What are you talking about?" I say.

"You decided to hole up with this? Was the night air too cold for you?"

Waya shuffles uncomfortably, saying nothing.

I shake my head. "That's not at all what happened!"

"Yeah, right!"

"I'm sorry Waya. You don't deserve to be put on the spot like this."

"And I do?!" My girlfriend kicks the basket against me. "You can pay for these and bring it back when you're ready to apologize!" She walks out.

I stare at the floor, trying to ignore onlookers.

A sigh comes from Waya. "Sorry, Leon… I don't mean to be a burden, but I really need to talk to you about what happened."

We sit outside in an alleyway on a couple of crates, undisturbed from locals. I had put the food back and apologized for the display.

"I've been looking all over for you in the woods. I didn't know you actually lived in this town."

"Yep, this is home as of a month ago. Where do you live?"

"In the wild."

She gets stranger all the time.

"How are you feeling?" Waya asks.

"How do you think I feel? Like complete crap. Misunderstandings are the kind of things she doesn't get over."

"No, I mean internally."

"Oh." I never gave it much thought beyond the previous night, but her inquiry brings a flurry of questions to mind. "Well, kind of hungry, because I haven't had an appetite for anything. I'm fatigued, too, even though I apparently got plenty of sleep the last couple of nights. I ended up sleeping the whole day away after I met you."

"Yeah, that's to be expected. You also didn't finish your meal."

"The leftovers I had packed were kind of bad, so I tossed the rest."

"Not that meal. The deer. Your scent was all over it."

"I thought you left that for me."

Her eyes narrow. "You hunted that yourself. I could tell by how it was handled."

My insides go cold. "With my bare hands?!"

She shakes her head. "No, during your first transformation."

"Okay, this is unreasonable. None of this is making any sense. And how do you even proclaim to know all of this? You're obviously a human like me."

Her eyes close. "If you freak out, I'm going to kill you here and now. Got it?"

The sudden bluntness beckons nothing more from me than a nod.

After looking around, Waya removes the headpiece, revealing a familiar-shaped snout, skin covered in unmistakable light grey pelage. She also takes off her gloves, showing arms just as furred, deadly-looking claws adorning her fingertips, albeit shorter than before. "Ugh, I don't enjoy wearing such restrictive clothing. At least the dress is loose enough."

Shocked, I'm left with little to say. "I'm not sure I follow."

"When I bit you, it's true that you contracted lycanthropy. You asked if you should be concerned about anything, and I was alluding to yourself."

"Aside from having to shave a couple times, I still look pretty normal."

"It happens over time. Anywhere from a few weeks to a couple of months. And of course, the slight protrusion to your face is inevitable as well. This is as far as it goes if you're not in werewolf form." Waya lightly brushes at her arms, the medium-thick fur moving aside for her fingers.

"You mean you can go between forms at will?"

"Sort of. It takes a lot of energy out of you to shift, and even after several years, I can't manage more than a few nights in a row at most. Though, I could maintain it indefinitely, if I so choose. Your wolf just needs to consistently feed to do so."

"Why aren't you in werewolf form now?"

She chuckles. "Like I told you before, it's hard to find game between the cold and competition from coyotes, bobcats and the like, so I scrounge or beg for what I can to go shopping."

"If I can change when I want, how come it happened the next night for me with no warning?"

"It was the moon. Three days of uncontrollable, total transformation for all werewolves when it's full, and it just happened to be on the final day for yours. Shifting also throws our hormones completely off-balance, usually resulting in ferocity. It takes serious time and focus to adjust. Since it was your first, that compounded, and you likely weren't even aware of what you were doing."

I lean back against a pallet. "This is a lot to take in."

"That's understandable. My first time wasn't so pretty."

"What happened?"

Waya replaces her gloves and niqab. "I don't want to talk about it. Anyway, you need to seriously reconsider your living arrangements. As I mentioned, this town is dangerous. People around here don't seem to appreciate a freak of nature." She leaves, disappearing beyond the corner.

Chapter 4

I sit for several minutes, considering Waya's words. From the sound of things, it seems I won't be acclimating to my surroundings for too much longer.

The sun begins to make its way down as I'm pacing, thinking about my life here. I definitely won't be getting a job, and there's no way my girlfriend would understand…

I could try to live on the streets, but all it would take is one person to notice me at the worst time, and I'd be done for.

No, Waya's right. There really is only one option left.

As I'm heading back to my place, I decide to make a big deal out of it. If there's one thing it seems my girlfriend understands, it's blunt behavior, so I might as well be forthright with her at a time like this.

The front door is unlocked, television growing louder as I step inside.

Heading straight for the bedroom, I don't bother saying anything, instead letting her have the first word, because I plan on getting the last.

She lowers the volume. "Leon, did you manage to get everything on the shopping list?"

I don't respond, stuffing my duffel bag with my looser clothing and a blanket.

Her voice grows louder as she walks into the room. "Hello?! Where are the groceries?"

"I didn't bother." I shove the dresser drawer shut and walk to the kitchenette, pulling a couple of bags and bottles of water from the refrigerator into a backpack.

"What do you mean you didn't bother? Hey, that's my lunch for tomorrow!"

I shut the fridge door and head into the bathroom, adding shampoo and toothbrush to my load.

"Leon, what the heck are you doing?!"

Staring at her, I grin. "Leaving."

"Leaving? You're supposed to be getting a job this week!"

"Nah, I don't think so." I head toward the front door, pulling it open.

My girlfriend shuts it hard. "Yeah? When are you coming back?"

I turn my head, crouching slightly to meet her eyes an inch away. I slowly advance as she backs against the wall, her breath shortening when she bumps into it, and I smile faintly with a whisper. "Never."

Feeling totally elated, I walk outside and pull the front door shut as gently as I can for maximum effect.

Stepping onto the sidewalk, I head off nonchalantly toward the edge of town, surprised at my own display of taking charge. It's unlike me to exhibit that sort of behavior, but she's pushed me too far over the past week, and I'm tired of it.

I don't doubt that she got the message, and if we ever do meet again, she'll think twice before treading on my mentality.

There's no way her actions will ever affect me again.

The night air is frigid, so I slip on the thick sweater, glad to have packed extra clothes. I drape the blanket around my shoulders, storing up good warmth for myself. Extra fur has apparently started growing in random spots along my body, so the cold doesn't bite into me as much. Still, it might be a bit before I'm as covered as Waya.

Fortunately, I never have to worry about shaving again.

The forest draws near. I stop at the tree line, staring into the greenery. I've never been one to think about roughing it in the wilderness, and don't have much in the way of camping experience, but if this is what must be done, then so be it. This town won't be keen on accepting me or any other werewolves with open arms.

I sit on a nearby boulder, withdrawing a bite to eat. A tuna sandwich will have to suffice for the night, as we didn't have much food for me to pack. Good thing I love fish so much.

Begging is always an option, as Waya had suggested for herself. Chances are that since not a lot of others know me around here, I might try getting away with it. With how much hair is growing on my face, I very well could pass for a bum. At least for a couple of days, if need be.

I look up to the sky, a waning gibbous staring back down upon the world. According to what was mentioned, involuntarily becoming a full werewolf again shouldn't be a worry for almost a month. That'll provide enough time to hole up away from everyone else.

Once again, I find myself traipsing the trails of the wild, only this time it was my choice. Oddly enough, I feel at peace about it. I have absolutely no idea what I'm going to do with my time out here, but the pressures of modern living situations are off my shoulders, so that helps. I think I'd rather be hunting for food than washing dishes, anyway.

The sun is gone from my view, long shadows becoming solid pools of darkness that enshroud the land. The creatures of the night start to show, bringing a distant chorus all around. I don't hear any wolves yet, but I'm bound to at some point.

After another hour of mindless walking, I happen across a decline in the earth, leading into a shallow cave. It looks pretty natural, and there doesn't appear to be any sign of use.

I drop my belongings within and sit against one of the rough walls. Drawing the blanket over myself, I close my eyes and settle my mind from all the recent happenings. I knew moving to a new town would be eventful, but this is ridiculous.

Chapter 5

My eyes open to the light shining through the cave entrance. I didn't dream, but feel rested all the same.

Stretching with a yawn, I scratch at my arms, hair all the more noticeable. Only time will tell when it completely covers me in a thicker layer. It's a bit strange to think of myself covered entirely in fur, more so what color it just might take on. Waya appears as a light grey, but I highly doubt that's what her original hair color was.

When she uncovered her head, I didn't observe any actual hair. I suppose with fur, it's not really necessary. Still, it's going to take some getting used to.

I wonder how we're supposed to shift form at will. Sitting silently, I close my eyes and focus, thinking about the dream that apparently was reality. After a few minutes, I open my eyes, and find that nothing is any different.

"Well, no surprise there. I should ask her about it next time."

Emerging from my place of solace, the afternoon greets me with a slightly bitter chill of a breeze. I dig out another tuna sandwich and make quick work of it. Aside from my impromptu meal a few nights ago and a shoddy meatloaf dinner, I haven't had much. I decide to eat a little more of what I packed and head out for the day.

Weighing my choices before me, I casually saunter around the woods. Going into town could be helpful to try begging, but being around other people right now doesn't really appeal to me. It wasn't often I went out to socialize, but now my options are only going to become all the more limited.

Though... there is one thing I could really make use of at a time like this.

The industrial yard approaches, the sound of other voices shouting here and there as construction work is being done on a new facility.

I sneak up behind a trailer, listening intently for any signs of movement to get an idea of who's going where. I knew I had good hearing, but this is incredible!

While the men are going to and fro, I'm able to discern the slightest shuffling as boots kick up dirt and gravel. Closing my eyes, it's easy to imagine paths mapped out in my mind while listening to each individual.

At the perfect moment, I dash around the front and find a bag of tools. Less than half a minute later, I'm gone from the area. Sure, I feel bad about doing this, but I'll think of a way to make up for it.

I spent my time constructing a bit of a fortified front to the cave. It isn't much, but this makes things feel more like a home away from home than a random hole in the earth. It seems that watching those home renovation shows came in handy after all.

Proud of my rough but formidable work from a hard afternoon, I settle the tools and begin gathering loose wood and kindling, stockpiling everything into the cave to keep it out of any weather conditions bound to occur.

At first, the inevitable need to eat had me consider either begging, a local soup kitchen, or learning to make use of a bow, but then I realize that being a werewolf will bring its own perks in the hunting department. Despite Waya's mention of the lack of game to be found, I know it'll have to come to that eventually, so practice might as well come sooner than later.

Additionally, the thought of relying on others at this point really seems to bother me, and I'm not sure why. I don't hate other people, but playing the scenes out in my head really annoys me right now.

I clear my head of unneeded thought and work on building a small fire, evening's cold edging in. Fortunately, that bag had a nice box of flint to go with the steely tools. Not more than a few minutes later do I have a nice flare going.

Huddled near the fire, I'm chipping at a rock with a chisel to pass the time. Keeping myself entertained will be a challenge out here. Boredom doesn't easily become me, but no computer, television, or general outings on the town leave something to be desired.

"You know, you make it really easy to find you."

I startle and drop the stone, standing with a turn to be met with Waya's face, my feet almost stumbling over the log I was sitting on.

She laughs. "You need to work on being more inconspicuous."

This is the first time I'm seeing Waya fully in her normal form. She dons a navy criss-cross top and black, baggy cargo pants, a nice compliment to her lighter fur.

"How did you even get so close without me hearing?" I ask.

"You'll figure it out." Waya grins, walking around me to examine my craftsmanship, tracing a few fingers along the trimmed tree limbs. "Not bad for a makeshift home."

"Thanks. I figured to get settled with a semi-permanent lodge. I'll probably work on it more tomorrow."

"You left town pretty quickly. But then, I'm not really surprised."

My eyes narrow. "It wasn't *that* bad."

"Oh, I don't doubt it, but considering the circumstances, you likely wanted to be alone."

"How... how do you know that?"

She shrugs. "You're a guy."

I scoff. "Oh, that's not sexist at all."

"But it's true."

Her casual tone edges my nerves. "That doesn't mean anything!"

"Mm-hmm. Just admit it. You couldn't bother with the thought of getting help from anyone else, so made do with your own skills."

My mind feels exposed. "Shut up, Waya!"

"Make me."

Before I realize it, I jump at her, a hard blow out of nowhere to my face sending me to the ground. The sting of her claws bites into my skin, and I can't help but to lay on the ground, unsure of how to react.

Waya kneels down, reaching for my face. I try to push her hand away, but her grip is unrelenting. "Sorry," she whispers.

Taken aback by her sudden shift of stance, I sit up, confused. "I… no, I should be sorry. It's not like me to lash out like that."

"It is now." Drawing further on my confusion, she continues. "Like I said, you're a guy. This change is overthrowing your hormonal balance, so I expected you to take on a dominant position. The only reason I struck you was to break you out of it."

Understanding dawns on me like a rock to the head. When I close my eyes to try and clear my mind, I feel her tongue against my face.

"What the heck—"

"Come on, don't make me explain it again. Those cuts aren't going to heal well if I don't take care of it now."

I squint against her action, noticing an unusual length of tongue go to work. It's not exactly gross, considering all that I've witnessed thus far, but a few extra inches is still peculiar to me.

Just as it was with my neck, the wounds almost instantly start to heal, the pain half-gone.

"There, that wasn't so bad, was it?"

"No, but did you have to make my face so wet doing that?"

She laughs. "You're welcome. It's going to take a lot quicker now that you're also part-wolf, but you'd have been hard-pressed doing that yourself. Anyway, what are you going to do with your time out here?"

"That's what was on my mind right before you showed up. It's weird to think about a normal life, getting a job, living in a building, going shopping. All standard experiences on a regular basis, only to spend the next day entirely devoid of all that."

"Welcome to the new normal."

I look to her. "What do you keep busy with?"

With a sigh, Waya picks up a stick to poke at the kindling. "Not a lot, to be honest. I hunt for food when I can, making those excursions into town otherwise, and spend a great deal of time just wandering and relaxing in some of my favorite spots around the woods. When night falls, I eventually rejoin…"

Realizing she's already spoken too far, Waya continues, eyes closed in frustration. "I go back to my family."

"Oh, you have family around here?"

She sets her jaw. "I was adopted into a group of werewolves."

"That seems like a nice thing. To have fellow werewolves around."

"It would be," Waya breathes out with scorn, "but it's not easy trying to fit in with a new life like this. Seemingly caught between worlds with no actual choice in the matter. Feeling like you have nowhere to go, nobody to turn to… it's a lot to deal with all at once."

"At least it beats being alone."

"Yeah…"

"So, you said you were adopted?"

She stands back up. "I'd better head back now, but it was good seeing you again. Good night, Leon." Waya runs off into the depths of the night.

Chapter 6

A week has gone by since I established my cave home. My food supply was finished yesterday, and that was with considerable rationing.

I've attempted to figure out shifting over that time, but to no avail. If I don't succeed soon, it's going to be hard to manage food.

Waya hasn't been around, and I wonder if she's either forgotten about me, or decided to let me adjust to my new life alone. I recall her proving that a bit of dominance was beginning to take a hold on me, but the blow to my face pretty much subsided that feeling.

All in all, I wouldn't be surprised if she decided I'm better off left by myself.

Though a lot of skin is still showing, hair has grown in quite a bit thicker along my body, much to the disappointment of that on my head, which has been receding into a mass to accompany the rest of my face. Eventually, everything should balance out across my entire body, based from what I saw on Waya.

Regarding food, perhaps a fishing rod would have been an ideal option to take along. I ought to find a river in my travels for future use.

Feeling peckish, I decide to forage for whatever can be found, be it fruit, plant, or really anything edible.

Carrying a small load of various fruits and plants back to my cave, I see a familiar figure peeking in.

Doing my best to remain quiet, I sneak closer to her. Less than half a dozen yards away, she speaks. "A nice try, but still too noisy." Waya turns around, smiling.

"How did you hear me that time?"

"Your shoes. You're going to have to ditch those if you want to stay silent at all."

It dawned on me then that she never seems to be wearing shoes, the same relatively blunt claws as her fingers adorning her toes. "I'm guessing your feet toughen up, too?"

"Bingo." She glances at my bundle of rations. "Seriously? That's not going to cut it."

"It's the best I could find. That reminds me, I meant to ask you the last time we spoke, but I forgot to."

"Oh? What is it?"

"Exactly how do we shift?"

Waya smirks. "Still haven't figured it out, huh?"

"I wouldn't be vying with the forest for berries and herbs if I have."

"Good point. Well, I'll be the first to tell you that it isn't an easy concept to muster the strength for. At least, not the first couple of times."

"I'm sure I can handle it."

Waya rolls her eyes. "If you insist. You're going to have to feed your wolf to kick off the process."

"Meaning?"

"For starters, you need to ingest raw meat."

My face twitches lightly. "Oh."

"Told you. Believe it or not, your body has already become well-adapted to that. There's no risk, but there's no other way. It doesn't take much beyond the desire for fresh blood when you're experienced, but since you've never done it willingly before, you'll need the entire portion. A half-pound should do it."

I gape. "Got any suggestions to make it easier?"

"Nope."

"Now I understand why you go out of your way to shop in town when you can."

She nods. "If you're willing to allow me to draw off of you again, I'll grab you a red squirrel or something."

"But can't you shift without feeding?"

"Duh, but this makes it easier, and besides, I'm doing you a favor."

"This day is getting better every minute."

"Get over it, Leon," Waya says with a giggle. "This new life doesn't get any easier!"

Reluctantly, I hold out an arm, to which she grasps gently. "This may hurt a bit."

As teeth meet skin, I grimace, clenching my jaw hard, biting back an expected scream. Though, just as quickly as the pain surfaces, it begins to dull.

I rub at my arm, skin tingling as it usually does when healing from werewolf saliva. "That… hurt less than I expected it to. More pressure than pain."

"Your muscles and skin are toughening up. Bite your victims enough, and you'll be able to manage just as well in feeding. As I expressed before, killing your prey makes it harder to sustain yourself. Anyway, you might want to step back a bit."

As I give her extra space, she begins shifting, seemingly less grandiose than I imagined. Then, Waya starts writhing, involuntarily lashing out with her arms as her body contorts, heaving following suit.

I try not to describe the scene in my mind, choosing to close my eyes instead.

A brief minute later, I feel a claw tap on my arm. "Hey, I'm going to find something for you now. Don't make me waste my time, or I'll make you feed on yourself."

When she wanders off, I sit by the ashes of my fire pit, thinking about what raw meat could be like. It turns my stomach a bit, but also strangely appeals to me. Heh, maybe my wolf is getting hungry.

It doesn't take Waya long to find something. She runs back to the site, squirrel clutched in her mouth, which she drops at my feet.

Staring down at it, I'm unsure of whether or not I want to proceed.

"Leon..." An annoyed grunt emanates from her snout.

I pick up the squirrel and take out a knife from my tool bag. With a grimace, I begin to flay the carcass. "You know, this is a lot more appealing on nature shows."

When I'm finished, I bear the portion of meat, fresh as can be, eyes closed at the moment that's about to come.

"You'll adjust, Leon. I promise."

Her words do little to encourage me, but I raise it to my mouth anyway. Before it even reaches my lips, my heart quickens, breath shortening. I glance at Waya.

"I assure you, the reaction is normal," she says quietly. "You need to give in to that ravenous desire."

Without a second thought, I bite into the squirrel, a marginal taste soon becoming an insatiable hunger. By the time I'm finished eating, I feel like I'm going to burst, hands on my knees. I feel neither sick, nor disgusted, but rather inexplicably infuriated.

Waya crouches by my side, resting a hand on my shoulder. "I'll be here to guide you through it all."

I lower to the ground, grabbing at my sides as I feel my muscles contract, moving along with my limbs as everything starts to contort. Arms, legs, even my face takes on a more extreme physique.

My eyes change as well, vision getting hazy in the midst, and I yell out.

Claws dig into my arm. "Hey, you need to remain focused."

The words reverberate in my head, but make little sense. My hands grip at the dirt beneath me, wanting to tear the ground up.

"Leon, don't lose your mind!"

I wrench away from her grip, roaring at her face, and bolt off in the opposite direction, anxious to get away so I can eat after so long.

The female gives chase, but I refuse to let her steal my kill. It's mine!

She tackles be from behind, sending us both tumbling into a gully, dry brush and twigs flying around as we attempt to overthrow one another. This inferior wolf isn't going to best me!

I rip at her with my claws, catching her forearm, her retaliation marring my side. It stings, only making me angrier.

With all my might, I swing at her, knocking her to the ground, and once again make my way out into the heart of the forest, excited to taste my prey after almost two weeks of starvation.

***

Breathing out, the heat of a voracious appetite escapes me as I look around in confusion, the night woods encapsulating my presence to hide me from would-be competition.

Wait, competition? From what?

My forearms are resting on something soft, fur matted in streaks of blood. I sit up and rub my arms against my clothing.

Something coughs. I turn my head, alert toward the sound. Waya cocks a glance at me from a couple of yards away. "Done yet?"

"Done with what?"

"You were indulging in your kill for half an hour, probably savoring every bite."

Looking down at the deer, I sigh heavily. "Guess I lost control again…"

"It takes time to get used to shifting. You'll likely start to manage by the next full moon."

My mind flashes back to when I ate the squirrel. "Did I hurt you?"

Waya smiles. "Just a few scratches. But hey, you got a good few nights' worth of food out of it."

Chapter 7

After carrying the deer back to camp, I had begun to prepare it for cooking, working intently with concentration to distract my mind.

"Look, it's really not as bad as it was with your first time manually shifting. That part *does* get easier."

"But how am I supposed to get a kill out here for shifting if I have to shift first to get it? I'm not exactly skilled with a bow or a gun."

Waya shakes her head. "As I suggested, the desire for blood will be enough once you're experienced, but maybe I'm wrong, and you can learn to do it sooner."

"That desire to kill scares me."

"As it should." A sigh escapes her. "We've got a strong sense of whatever humanity is left in us, Leon. You're not going to go berserk and wind up killing anything that moves. You *are* going to adapt."

"Doesn't it ever scare *you*?"

"Yes. It scares me a lot sometimes. I still have nightmares."

I set one of the deer limbs over the fire. "How did you adjust?"

"My adoptive pack kept us fed, ensuring there was a fresh supply of raw game for me until I came to terms with my wolf. The leader knew there was no sense in trying to stifle that hunger. It doesn't matter how much you eat in your unshifted form, because eventually that wolf is going to want out. If not by the next full moon, then by force, and that is far worse."

My head nods in understanding. "Then I'd best keep it up whenever possible. Would it hurt to try and shift every night?"

Waya crosses her arms. "No, I don't think so. Some of our pack prefer to stay in wolf form almost all the time, provided there's enough meat to feed on. Remember when I said I could maintain my wolf indefinitely? On one occasion, I've been able to stay shifted for over a week, day and night. Our leader has been in his form since I was brought in. Not once have I ever seen him out of his wolf. He's an apparent exception to needing consistent feeding, so it must be possible with no consequence. Unless that's what you consider a downside." She grins.

Many thoughts continue to fight for voicing, but one in particular has settled since earlier this afternoon. "Where did you go over the past week?"

Grin becomes frown, and I'm unsure whether she looks like she wants to shout or cry. "My pack forbade me to return. After your scent became more noticeable, everyone became decidedly harsh against me. Some thought I was abandoning the pack, while others believed me to try and take over. Despite my assurances, most still fear any others knowing of us."

"But I'm a werewolf now, aren't I?"

"Only recently. Besides, we've all been together for a long time. You're still by far considered a stranger. It'll be bad enough that I decided to return here at all. Chances are I'll end up getting in a fight with a few over it."

"It doesn't have to be that way, though. Your pack can be made to see reason, that not everyone else has to be an enemy."

"Nevertheless, my pack seems to think it's safer this way. I'm the only one that goes near the town at all, much less the only one who kept in touch after feeding off another human."

"Everyone must think you're brave for doing that." I hand her a raw cut of the deer, which she accepts.

"Thanks. And yes, I'm thought of as both brave and stupid."

"Sorry to hear that. I'll understand if you have to stay away."

"Eh, don't be. It isn't your problem. And I won't let my pack tell me where I can or can't go. That's my decision."

"Thank you for teaching me how to shift. I promise to keep practicing when I can."

Waya shrugs, working over a bite of meat. "That's up to you. Learning to shift on demand and controlling your wolf is only going to be helpful, both in hunting and keeping its hunger in check. Not to mention it can be a lot of fun," she finishes with another grin.

Later that night, I go out for more prey. Waya was right that a desire for blood would be sufficient, because I have no problem shifting almost immediately. She'll be impressed!

When my prey is found, I kill it swiftly, a last breath drawn by the bobcat as my sharp teeth puncture deeply into flesh.

"Pretty good, Leon, but still not good enough." Waya pounces on me from behind before I know it, her claws scratching at me furiously. "I need to eat, too!"

"It's my kill, Waya! I'm not sharing." I bite at her face, missing her by an inch.

"You might've learned to shift so quickly, but I'm more experienced by ten years!" She retaliates, tearing at my neck, and I surrender the kill, taken aback by her sudden change.

"Waya… why are… you doing this…?"

She stands over me, grinning fiercely. "Because I was starved, Leon, and you were dumb enough to make yourself vulnerable. I won't be locked up any longer!"

Waya seizes my neck, and my vision is gone.

Opening my eyes in a panic, I roll over, seeing nobody else around. I check my neck, and find that there's no trace of damage.

I attempt to fall back asleep, shivering from fear.

Chapter 8

"It... it hurtsss..." My statement becomes increasingly difficult to form as my face shifts.

"I know, but just keep pressing into it. Soon, you won't feel a thing."

Waya grips my wrists as my hands cramp, tendons stretching to accommodate semi-retractable claws. My sides heave as my organs shift around and muscle becomes layered, leaving me nigh breathless.

Her claws dig into my furred skin harshly, keeping me grounded in the shift so I can focus my thoughts. It's an odd method, but effective.

I collapse to the ground, my eyes stinging as I attempt to ignore the pain. Then, everything becomes numb, the tingling pressure of the dirt pushing against me as I glance up.

Drawing a clawed hand to my face, I examine every angle, feeling my surroundings in an entirely new perspective. *Incredible...*

"Isn't it an amazing feeling?"

The power... The sheer power! I take several deep breaths, flooding my sense with the woods, trails of movement and fresh game mapping out in my mind. Given mere seconds, I could easily close the space between any one of my chosen targets without trouble.

It's been three nights after my recent manual shift, two of which I spent in contemplation and cooked meat. By the mid-afternoon of today, Waya appeared once again, asking me of my decision. I just couldn't bring myself to try again in the meantime, but felt very strongly of success with her being here.

She had no trouble finding me something small after drawing off of me once again. A quarter-pound of vole later, I'm as big as she is, only a little bulkier.

I glance into the nearby puddle from today's light shower, a dark grey visage staring back. Waya stands beside me, her lighter fur sharply contrasted suddenly, her golden eyes staring into my deep blue as the water ripples from a breeze.

"So, which animal caught your attention first?"

"Huh?" I say, astonished.

A smirk appears on her face. "I know you could sense each one near here, so tell me what you noticed."

I allow my mind to clear, focusing on the very first hint of movement in my ears as I continue adjusting to speaking with a muzzle. "It was a… deer. No, an elk." My eyes flash open. "How…?"

"You caught on to shifting surprisingly quick, believe it or not. Your wolf also has a lot more going for him than you think."

"Speaking of which, I think he's hungry."

Waya leans in a bit, a quiet voice between her teeth. "Then what are you waiting for? Let's hunt."

Without delay, I run off to track the ungulate, Waya following closely behind. It doesn't take long before I find my prey, and I ready myself to move in for the kill. He notices too late, and makes a feeble attempt to escape as Waya and I box him in.

For once, I'm glad that this female knows her place… she'll help me take it down, and then I feast!

Waya and I attack, bringing the elk down quickly. The fresh scent of meat is overwhelming, and as soon as I finish him off, I snarl at her, swinging a clawed hand wildly.

"Whoa, calm down, Leon! I'm not going to take your kill."

I stare intently at her, confused as to why she wouldn't want my prey. Does she not think me worthy to fight over it?!

Shaking my head, I breathe out as though I just ran ten miles. "Waya, I... I'm sorry. My wolf... he thought you... were competition."

"Don't worry about it. I know that you're only starting to get a good hold on your wolf, so I don't need to fight him."

"Thanks. Here... come and have some."

Waya flinches lightly. "No, I... can't. You deserve to indulge in your first controlled kill. It's enough of an honor to witness it."

"Are you sure?"

"Yes. You earned the sustenance for your time out here, and besides, my pack will do well enough to keep us fed."

I take the carcass back to my site, content with the ability to now shift under control. Bearing an abundance of meat that I can ration eases my nerves for settling into the wild, and having a good acquaintance helping me learn how to manage my fate is reassuring.

Back in my normal form, I work at the meat, cutting it to store and set for cooking, a healthy fire casting a myriad of shadows around.

"I'm curious, Waya. Why did you say that you can't have any of this? You had no problem accepting some of the deer I got last time. I'm not buying the whole 'deserved kill' thing."

Her jaw moves a bit, as though she's grinding her teeth. "No, it's just that... a couple of werewolves only share a collaborative kill for one reason... to become mates. It's the male that offers to the female that assisted him with the kill, so some females tend to vie for hunting experience."

"Oh, I see." I stare at the ground, thinking quickly of something else to discuss. "How many are in your pack?"

"Eleven of us, including the lead. I was the last one, and it's been that way for more than ten years."

"Wow, no wonder you're so skilled at this."

Waya laughs. "Yes, I've been a part of many hunts as we've traveled over the years. We settled in the state about two years ago, and have been in this forest ever since."

"Thank you again, Waya, for helping me to learn how to control my shifting. I feel like everything will be a lot easier to handle out here with such an ability."

"We do have that strength over your average human. Just remember to keep your wolf fed, and he'll respect you, making the form a lot more symbiotic. We've seen some werewolves who unfortunately thought total control is a given, only to fall victim to such a feral ferocity bringing early demise."

"It sounds like a nasty way to go."

"It is. One of our pack in earlier years decided he could try to reintegrate back into society. I'll just say that he finally lost control near a military training area. Like we needed that kind of exposure…"

"Huh, I don't recall seeing anything about that in my research."

"That's the government for you. Still doesn't help knowing some people with that kind of power know about us."

I nod. "Have you ever lost control?"

She straightens up, shifting her gaze minimally before looking back at me. "I should be getting back to my pack. You take care of yourself, Leon. I'll check on you again some time."

Chapter 9

A new day is set before me, overcast and slightly drizzling an icy rain, excess humidity and cold roiling my senses as I come to.

After spending a good deal of time with Waya the other day learning to control my shifting, I don't really feel like getting up. Nevertheless, it wouldn't do me any good just lazing around, so I decide to start my day with a hearty meal.

Elk shank set out before me, I begin to work on a fire in the overhang, but quickly decide that I might just prefer it raw this time.

This was definitely the right choice.

Raw muscle, satiating to my tongue...

So unusual, this texture.

Never enough... give me more.

It's strange, but satisfying...

Glad that female isn't here to steal my share...

No, she's not here to challenge you. She's... she's...

My eyes open, a deep breath filling me before I exhale, the wondrous scents and signals a buffet for indulgence.

Wait a minute…

Trespassers. Encroaching on my territory!

My head snaps up, ears totally alert to the most minute sounds. A faint rustle of leaves…

Bang!

A gunshot echoes into the surrounding trees, deadly vibration reverberating in my head. Before I can even grasp what just happened, my wolf tears off with mad haste.

My legs blazing from the surge of adrenaline, I can't get a grasp on my own thoughts.

Coming for me!

No, wait, what…?

Run, now!

I decide to allow him to control the immediate course of action as he leads me away from a perceived threat, and only then do I start to hear distant voices.

"Was that a bear, man?"

"No, there's no way that was a bear, Too scrawny. It was… more like a wolf."

"What? That thing was huge! Wolves don't get *that* big!"

"I'm gonna kill it, then. Might be an interesting trophy. It'll make up for my lack of buck meat this past year."

Huh? Hunting season doesn't go this long.
Escape! Run, run, run!
No!

My claws dig into the hard, cold dirt as I skid to a sudden halt.

Death! Retreat! No, not—I—
Shut up!

I grip at my head, nails prickling my temples.

"Dude, it's going crazy! We should leave it alone, man."

"No way! Something that weird deserves to die."

Another gunshot blares, sound boring through my head. My wolf can barely contain himself, vicious urges ripping at my consciousness.

Unable to contain it any longer, the driving force fills me with an inundant fury, roar bellowing from my lungs. My eyes flash in the direction of the voices, breath out of control as my heart quakes with both fear and rage.

With what feels like nothing more than a second, I burst from the trees, claws outstretched at my prey. The hunter becomes hunted, as he collapses to the ground, shrieking from my sudden change of direction.

I roar directly at his face, and he faints from the onslaught of sheer terror. This guy was no threat to me, but then where...

Just as I lose interest from the lack of a challenge, another bullet shatters my focus, a gash stinging my shoulder.

Finally, something worth killing!

My assailant goes to fire another round at me, and I violently pounce at him, shoving him into a tree.

When I regain my footing, cold steel is pressed against my face, handgun barrel staring me point-blank between my eyes. Holding my breath for a heart-stopping moment, I see him pull the trigger.

Click.

Grinning, I go to press my claws against his neck, minor traces of blood appearing.

All of a sudden, he slams the handgun against the side of my head and pulls away, my nails taking a bit of flesh from him as he retreats.

Dizzy from the blow, I give out a harsh bellow, trying to regain focus. I lose sight of the man, his trail disappearing rapidly in the freezing rain.

My claw rips at the tree in frustration, sending bark splinters out from the trunk. *My prey got away!*

No, he wasn't prey, but he was an enemy.

Left cold and unfulfilled, I wander back to my site and shift out, content with sleeping the rest of the day away.

***

The following evening welcomes me as I lazily rise from my den cave, happy with the excess sleep with little else to consider for the time.

Before I manage to make it fully outside, someone sidesteps in front of me, halting me in my tracks half-crouched. "Oh, Waya, how's—"

She jams a finger in my face, sending me backward onto the ground as I shimmy away, her steps following me right back into the cave, my back bumping against the wall as she shouts. "Leon, you idiot! How could you do something like that?!"

"Hold on, what do y—"

"I leave you alone for *one day* after you learn to control your shifting, and you go berserk?!"

"What are you talking about?"

Waya throws her head back in an irritated groan, proceeding to stare me down. "You attacked a couple of random guys just going for a walk!"

"Whoa, wait a second! One of those guys shot at me!" I want to stand back up and shove her out, but my developed sense of respect for her keeps me on the floor.

"Shot at you?" Her brows furrow, considering my words intently. "That's *not* what I heard."

"Heard? From who?"

With an exhaled snort and crossed arms, I'm given a rundown. "Only two-dozen or so townsfolk. I went shopping yesterday evening, and between the begging and browsing, I had to listen to all the varying rumors revolving around the incident, but most agreed that it was your fault."

I frown. "I'm not surprised."

"Neither am I." Waya turns around. "I had a feeling things were blown out of proportion. Any half-wit wouldn't be dumb enough to admit picking on a werewolf. But then... I don't actually recall the word 'werewolf' being mentioned, so who knows exactly what he said originally?"

"I'm really sorry, Waya. I'll admit that I lost some control, but not until I was provoked!"

She turns back to me. "No, don't worry about it. I know that you're not the one to start a fight. You're too honest for that." A frown appears. "You need to be more careful. I was worried… not just for you, but for all of us."

"I'll try to stay out of the way of other humans."

Waya sighs heavily. "That's all I could ask, Leon. But, it isn't safe here anymore."

"You already told me the town wasn't safe."

"I don't mean that. I mean this part of the woods. Chances are likely that this guy is going to try and bring the authorities here. You might've lucked out with a gun, but against a squad? Not happening."

"Then, what do you suggest?"

She shuffles aimlessly for a minute, staring around at the trees as though someone might be stalking us. "My pack. I'm hoping that everyone will be open to the idea of bringing you in. I'll just have to persuade the others that you can pull your own weight, that you're not gonna sap off us like an invalid."

"I'm glad you have that much confidence in me."

"Don't sell yourself short. You're still new at this, but more capable than you'll know in even a year from now."

"If you say so." I get off of the cave floor and walk back outside. "When should we leave this place?"

"At nightfall. Nobody's going to come out here right now, much less in the dark, but tomorrow is asking for trouble. My pack is far enough as it is, so that shouldn't be a problem for the town."

"How far will we be going?"

"All I can say is that you'd better load up on as much elk as you can. I already ate this afternoon, so I'll be fine."

"Won't the leftovers be an issue?"

"Your scent is already all over here. Nothing you can do about that. We just need to go far and fast in an hour."

I finish off a large portion of the remaining store of meat, Waya offering little in terms of conversation. Once the last sliver of sun disappears behind the barren limb-filled horizon, we both shift and head out into the deep darkness of the forest.

Chapter 10

The muted patter of our steps descend into the woodland, the heat of our breath sounding as we cross several miles of foreign terrain. I knew that forests could be big, but this is incredibly daunting. Nonetheless, despite the sheer amount of ground we've covered together, I don't feel too tired. Rather, I'm excited to see more of this world beyond what I've known.

To anticipate my integration with our fellow werewolves—others who've suffered a like fate in one way or another—will be reassuring that I needn't go about it alone. Even though I'm abandoning almost everything I've learned, I feel more prepared than ever before, and I have Waya to thank for that.

She still seems kind of distant much of the time, but if anything, I personally consider her a friend. I'd respect her for putting her pack first, but just the willingness to introduce me feels like an honor. I'll be sure to put my best intentions forward.

We begin to slow down after what felt like a small eternity, the frozen ground only now becoming noticeable against my feet. The wolf's sensitive pads begin to observe the vibrations coming from a couple of directions.

"Leon, shift out."

Without hesitation, I do so, knowing that my trust is in her hands no matter what form I'm in. She follows suit almost immediately, our bodies reforming to the bipedal form we've now come to know.

As her clothing resettles and light grey fur contracts with muscle, I glance at myself while I do the same. Only, this time, my skin is barely visible, dark grey now covering most of what's exposed. I roll up my sleeves to merely prove what I can feel, medium fur beginning to take over my standard human body. Now that I think about it, the more I shift to and fro, the more my wolf's fur stays.

The vibrations in the ground are slightly less noticeable, but continue to grow as whatever is headed our way nears.

I close my eyes and inhale deeply to recuperate, and to take in the various scents suddenly amplified.

There are eight, nine… ten others, all approaching at once. Just as I open my eyes, the beings start to form along the silhouetted trees to my north and east.

My eyes stay on Waya, who appears motionless. Her focus barely catches my eyes for a fraction of a second, expecting me to follow her lead. I refuse to move a muscle until she does, so as not to display uncertainty or fearful retreat. This is her pack's territory, and I'm not going to force myself upon it.

Waya kneels down, as do I. One of the other werewolves meanders over to her, staring down with a glare, before hitting her. I want to go over and help her up, but my wolf is rooted in absolute deference.

She allows herself to stay on the ground for a few seconds, then slowly rises to her feet to stare straight back into the eyes of her attacker.

He speaks bluntly. "You were gone all day again, Waya."

"I needed to be, Locan. The pack needs extra rationing."

"You ask me, and then I tell you when you can go out! I'm the leader for a reason!" Locan's words are direct and unforgiving.

"The hunting's been bad. You know that's why I do this."

He huffs. "We've been through harder times…"

"Why do we keep subjecting ourselves to hunger? It doesn't hurt to be more resourceful!"

"*Not* with the humans! It's getting worse, Waya. I don't want any more wolves dying to murderous hands over food!"

She yells back. "If not by human hands, then by starvation!"

Locan looks as though he's about to strike again, but another werewolf interrupts, his snickering echoing in the silence. "Maybe she'd be better off living with the humans. More for us."

"Silence, Tano, or I'll feed you to our pack."

"Um, Locan," another one says, her voice hesitant.

"What is it, Kemalu?"

She points to me, at which Locan averts his attention, stepping over to investigate. "What… who are you? *Speak!*"

I try to find my voice in the sudden outburst. "I—I'm—"

Looming figures of anthropomorphic terror close in all around me, my ears filled with heavy breathing.

A grin emerges from one of the shadowy visages. "A willing meal, the way I see it." He flashes deadly, white fangs with a growl.

The thought of being fought over, only to be ripped apart in the end leaves me unsettled, but I remain perfectly still, passively looking to each set of eyes piercing my being.

"You eat enough as it is, Tilan!" says another wolf.

"Back off, Manita! I don't care if you're the leader's daughter, he's mine!" Tilan leaps for me, but gets shoved aside by Locan.

"Until I find out what's going on, nobody is eating this—" He crouches slightly, looking closer at my face. "… What *are* you?"

"I… I'm a werewolf, like you."

Locan stares intently, then laughs, turning to step away a few feet. "This pup thinks he's just like me." He turns back around. "When did you contract?"

"A little over a couple weeks ago."

"How long have you been shifting by choice?"

"Uh, for a few nights now."

"How many were under total control?"

"… Two."

He stands straight, snorting at my pitiful excuse for being a werewolf. "You've got guts. I'll say that I'm marginally impressed you managed control in so little time. You should leave us before you get hurt." Locan addresses Waya. "Did you bring him here?"

"Yes. I thought that he would be good help for the pack."

The other wolves make an array of noises, anything from gasps to exclamations, jeers to growls.

The leader stamps a foot, bringing everyone quiet. "He isn't one of us. How can you trust him?"

"He has experience with modern society. He knows more about the local town than any of you!"

"He's still too human to even be out in the wild. For all you know, he'll betray us."

Waya shouts. "You don't understand! He's not like any other so-called civilian!"

"I will *not* hear of it! If you don't send him away, I'll take care of the situation myself..." Deadly claws gleam in the moonlight.

She swallows hard. "No... you can't do this!"

The large hand strikes hard on her jaw, sending her against a tree, thin streaks of blood appearing on her face. Her mouth is contorted visibly by sheer hatred, eyes hidden in shadow, a faint tear trickling downward. Whether it's out of pain or pity, I can't tell.

Locan steps up to her, grabbing her face in both hands, claws fully extended. "Did you bite him?"

"..."

"Waya!" He screams. "Did. You. Bite him?"

"... Yes."

He drops his hands, claws retracting partly. "After all I did for you... you go and feed on a human." The leader looks at her with disgust and resentment. "He's your mess. You can clean up after it." Locan then walks back amongst the remainder of the pack. "Let her die with the prey."

For the first time, I see Waya begin to cry, fury flaring within me. Before I'm even fully shifted again, I feel myself running at Locan, tackling him just as he starts to turn toward me.

I claw at him, leaving a couple of cuts behind while we roll a couple of yards. We stand up and I seize him again. He wrenches an arm at me, grabbing me by the throat. His fingers start to crush, halting my growl instantly, tears drawing from my eyes.

He whispers just audibly enough for me to hear. "I don't care who you think you are. Breathe anywhere near me again, and I *will* kill you. *Painfully.*"

No sooner than his hand relaxes do I slip to the ground almost unconscious, afraid to even think about breathing.

Locan walks away in silence, retreating into the forest, the pack following without a single word.

Chapter 11

A half hour went by before Waya or I said anything to each other, but it felt like so much longer since the pack left. I had tried to clean her wound, but she shoved me back, refusing to allow me near.

With her silent treatment done, she wipes at her eyes. "You're an idiot, Leon."

I don't respond, thinking anything I could possibly conceive would make things all the worse.

"Thank you for standing up to Locan, by the way. I've been wanting to do that for a couple of years."

Now confused, I can't help but to speak. "I'm sorry."

"Don't be, please. This was bound to happen sooner or later. Like I said, it's been over a decade. Locan's made a lot of sacrifices for everyone, especially me."

The inevitable question resurfaces. "How did you get adopted into his pack?"

She resettles herself upon the boulder, eyes unfocused and distant toward the ground. "It was about two weeks after I contracted lycanthropy. I had wandered out one night during a hot summer, admiring a beautiful, starry sky. I wasn't paying attention and made my way near the woods. Movement had caught my attention, beckoning me to investigate.

"By the time I realized what it was, it was too late. The werewolf attacked me, leaving a deep cut in my arm. When I made it back home, I was brought immediately to the hospital. After being thoroughly evaluated, I was recommended to a particular specialist. The doctor that saw me had experience treating a couple of other patients who suffered a werewolf attack, demanding that we keep quiet about it if he treated me. He explained the situation, providing some information about symptoms and keeping my wolf tended.

"Despite this, my parents felt that it could be suppressed, believing that it would eventually go away. Though I protested, I was kept out of school and inside our home every day, away from everyone else. I wasn't ever allowed to play outside anymore, and none of my friends were allowed to come over."

"That must've been extremely difficult on you."

"It was, and my parents and sister didn't have an easy time trying to box me and my wolf in. I wasn't even allowed to eat any sort of meat. I was alive, but I wasn't able to live. A kid can only enjoy her video games and books so much.

"One night, my family sat down for a round of steaks. I was locked in my bedroom, but the scent was overwhelming. I beat my fists at the door, being ignored the whole time. Then, it happened. My body shifted for the first time since I was attacked, my wolf uncontrollable. I tore down the door and..."

Waya clutches at her head in agony, tears streaming relentlessly.

I try to offer some form of comfort, but beyond a simple side-hug, there's little I can think of. "Were your parents and sister badly injured?"

"Leon, I *killed* everyone!"

My body tenses, the cold air no longer a bother as my own skin freezes from such terror, but I won't shy away from her. The last thing she needs is additional abandonment. No doubt that the trauma of her incident caused a lot of stress, obviously inducing a form of amnesia regarding her name and probably some other things as well.

Stability is the best form of medicine sometimes, and that's what she's going to get.

"I'm a danger to everybody… I can't do anything right."

"Waya, you didn't kill me."

"But I inflicted you with this wretched curse!"

"You also showed me how to take control, and to make the most of it."

She sniffs, pouting under her breath. "I'm so sorry, Leon."

"You have nothing to be sorry for, Waya. You didn't ask to contract lycanthropy, and you didn't beckon your family to suppress your wolf. And you certainly didn't want your pack to leave you behind."

"What am I going to do…?"

I sigh out. "I don't know, but you're strong. You've got to do what you can to press on. I'm not going to give up, so neither should you."

Waya breathes heavily, sitting silently for a moment. "You're right. I'm still me, pack or no pack."

"Maybe we can head back toward the town. We can still make use of extra food then."

"I dunno… maybe it isn't safe to hang around there at this time. Are you sure it's a good idea?"

My shoulders slump. "I'm not really sure about anything anymore, to be honest. But, I can say that I have a friend to keep me company while I figure it out."

"Can't disagree with you there. You're the only one who's treated me like a friend, instead of an asset."

"Should we go back now to see if it's alright?"

Waya sighs, still leaning into me. "No, I just need to sleep."

We both take to the ground, finding rest as we fall asleep in the quiet night.

***

It's mid-afternoon when we awaken, a lukewarm day to stave off the recent bitterness in the air.

Waya is still sleeping, so I let her be while I shift into my wolf, setting out for a decent breakfast. A short time into the hunt, I come across a couple of hares looking for food. Snatching up both one after another doesn't take long.

I bring my kills back to where we slept and leave one beside my friend while I devour the other, fresh game sating my wolf completely, the stress of last night's encounter starting to dissipate from my mind.

When done my own meal, I shift out, sitting near Waya to await her day's beginning.

It doesn't take too long for my kill to broach her senses, bringing her out of the deep sleep. "Wha... rabbit?" She grabs the lump of fluff, drawing it against her face like a pillow.

I can't help but chuckle. "You're supposed to eat it, not cuddle it."

She lays still for a moment, breathing in the aroma deeply, then bites into it, rending fur and flesh to nip at the sweet succulence within.

"Hope it starts you off well enough."

Waya finishes with a mouthful, breathing out in gratification. "Yes, thank you, Leon." She sits up, taking in the temperate air of the pleasant afternoon, kneading her claws toward the sky.

"So, what'll we do for the day?"

She brings her legs up, arms settling upon her knees as she thinks to herself. "I don't know. Everything about my life was organized and settled for the most part up until the other night. I had a sense of purpose, a role to play in my pack, and now... it's gone."

"You can make a new purpose for yourself."

Waya stares hard at me. "You don't know what it's like to belong to a different family for so many years. I've gotten used to fitting in to the routine of everyone else's life. Even going out and about on my own so often, I still actively considered the well-being of my packmates. It's kind of dumb to think about, but this is too much freedom. I feel almost useless."

She's got a point, in a sense. I don't know what life was like for her all these years, but she's got a strong personality, one that's worth using to the best of her ability.

"You've got a lot going for you, Waya. It's true when you say that I can't possibly empathize with your situation, but I know that life is more manageable with you around. I'd be totally lost if it weren't for your guidance."

"Oh, c'mon Leon, you aren't completely clueless about life."

I clear my throat, saying nothing.

"Wow, you really are, aren't you?" She sighs, shifting her demeanor as smoothly as she can her wolf. "Look, don't feel bad about it. Making a life for yourself is hard. Don't even get me started about trying to manage when a wrench is thrown into it, rendering everything you knew pointless.

Nobody plans for needing to survive alongside wolfish tendencies, that's for sure."

Chapter 12

Another week's gone by since Waya's pack deserted her. She couldn't sense any sign of the werewolves returning, and so tried to make peace with that. Nevertheless, I can see the pain it's caused her, to the point where she becomes irritable at times for seemingly no reason. There were a few nights that I could've sworn I heard her crying herself to sleep, but I wouldn't dare mention my knowledge of that.

Even though she's highly skilled in hunting, Waya has been unable to focus on our excursions. My own lack of experience isn't helping much, but even when she blames me, I don't say anything. Pointing out her flaws isn't going to benefit either of us, especially when food is on the line.

It also began to start snowing here and there since yesterday, making the season feel like it'll last even longer. Frosty days and freezing nights do not encourage our would-be meals to come out and play.

"Waya, it's okay. We're bound to find a good kill by the end of the week."

"No, Leon, it really isn't." She sits upon a log, hands to her head. "I don't need to let my wolf go hungry just because prey is hard to find. She can't handle trying to live off of measly feedings. I'm killing the next thing that comes our way."

Waya drops to the ground, beginning her shift. I do the same, thankful for the extra fur and toughened hands.

I've been able to practice shifting a few more times, the last one being done with no meat at all. Even Waya was astonished by this, expressing that I've taken to my wolf pretty quickly from what she's been told over the years by her former packmates.

As I shift now, it feels almost completely natural, as though I couldn't imagine what life was like before, and it's only been a little over three weeks. Even still, it takes me at least a few minutes to complete my form.

"C'mon, Leon, hurry up. I'm hungry…"

"I'm trying."

"Ugh, I'm going on ahead. Catch up when you're done." She runs off, anxious to feed her wolf.

With a sigh, I continue, hoping to not wind up disappointing Waya as we hunt down whatever we cross this evening.

When I'm done, I sprint in the direction we're headed, quickly picking up on her trail as she winds through the trees. Then, I'm aware of another batch of scents, all similar to one another.

My heart picks up pace as do my legs, my stride lengthening as I barrel towards what I hope isn't a confrontation.

"Leon, where are you? Help me!"

As I near, I see Waya backing up against a couple of trees, a band of six coyotes trying to close her in. Before anyone can take notice, I charge forward, pouncing on one.

He snaps at me, attempting to struggle out, but I bash at his face, knocking him unconscious. His mate breaks off from the others, her fangs bared as she leaps into me. I suffer a bite on my shoulder before sending her flying against a tree with a whimper.

When I'm able to reach Waya, she has three of the others taking turns biting at her legs, the fourth trying to lock onto her neck.

I let out a roar, startling a few of Waya's predators long enough for her to break free, leaping clear to join my side. She grasps at the coyote attached to her, tearing a bit of fur from his back before he decides to run off.

The remaining three rush us both, claws and teeth gnashing out of desperation, oblivious to the odds at this point. The onslaught comes to a quick end as we fight back, leaving two dead before us. We take one each, grateful for a decent meal.

Waya didn't take long to eat her coyote, myself a few mere bites in as she relaxes on the ground, tending to her wounds. "Thank you, Leon. I'm sorry for running ahead of you. I really should know better."

"Don't be too hard on yourself. You're the one that told me we gotta keep our wolves fed."

"Yeah, but I still could've waited two extra minutes. I was being stupid!" She punches the ground, reopening a wound.

I set my prey down and sit by her side, licking at the cuts in her neck as she tries to close the one on her hand again.

She sighs heavily. "Sorry. I've just been so upset that my own pack left me. It's been hindering my ability to hunt well, and I'm letting you down in the process."

"So I've noticed. For the record, you're not letting me down, Waya. I'm faring a lot better than I would be if I remained at my cave, not to mention the fact that I wouldn't be nearly as practiced with shifting."

"I suppose." Her eyes glance up at the moon, waxing gibbous shining brightly above as snowflakes silently descend upon the woods. "Only a few more nights before your first full, total shift. Hope you're prepared."

"Me, too." I return to eating, thinking deeply about the approaching event. "What's it like, shifting uncontrollably for three whole days?"

Waya ponders for a moment before speaking. "I've never really had to explain it before. It's kind of strange to experience your first time. Remember when you learned to shift the third time, and your wolf thought I was trying to steal your prey?"

"Yeah."

"Well, it's kind of like being caught in the mind of your wolf without your consent, but you're still completely aware of everything. You act of your own volition, but nothing is decided apart from your wolf's thoughts and desires on everything. It's one of the reasons you want to keep him fed and happy, because he'll come back to bite you then if not.

"It's the symbiotic relation I was talking about before. Give your wolf what he wants, and he'll give you what you want, plain and simple. His power and senses for your control and logic. It's a total win with proper respect."

I work at my kill, seemingly hungrier with every bite. "Hopefully I'm treating my wolf right."

She smiles. "Without a doubt."

Chapter 13

The warmth of sunlight rests upon my side as I come to, snow diminished around me from my body heat. This day is strangely temperate, and very welcome.

I glance over at Waya, her sleeping form sprawled along the ground, pine needles and leaves shoved aside at various angles, as though she couldn't get comfortable last night. Hopefully she's at least finding decent sleep.

As though she might've heard my thoughts, Waya opens her eyes, golden orbs peering at me as she goes to yawn, sitting up. "What?"

"Nothing. I was just wondering if you slept okay."

"I guess. What about you?"

"Sleeping on the ground has been surprisingly comfortable. It's no king-sized mattress of foam, but it's pretty good."

She smirks, shaking her head. "I can't remember my own bed from so long ago, though I doubt if I'd enjoy it anyway all these years later."

I look up at the trees, expecting to hear birds on a fair day like this, but as winter would have it, there's total silence.

Waya stands up suddenly. "Hey, wanna go for a swim? I know of a great, little swimming hole nearby. It's even got a waterfall!"

Before I can contemplate her question, she gets up and starts shifting, sounding notably happier than she has in the past week. I decide to tag along unquestioning, beginning to feel my own wolf emerge. Ready to go, we run off for wherever this swimming spot may be.

As we near the water, I see Waya wander over to a boulder near the edge, stripping off her cross top while she comes to a halt. When finished removing her cargo pants as well, she steps back toward the swimming hole, then looks at me. "What are you waiting for? Let's go!" Anxious grin alighting, Waya jumps in, launching streaks of water onto the ground.

Though some of our features are significantly less-defined in wolf form, I'm still unsure whether or not my clothes would benefit from a quick dip. Of course, Waya doesn't seem to care at all. She certainly didn't mind when I first met her, and I hadn't noticed a hint of her form until she spoke.

"You're not going to swim in your clothing, are you, Leon? Probably not a good idea, even if the day isn't as cold." She dives, tail following under with a flip of the water.

Point settled, I figure to leave my clothing by hers so I don't lose track of where it is. It's admittedly a bit awkward, but I jump in with no further thoughts on the matter.

Instead of an icy flash, I'm met with a strange cooling sensation, water rushing across my thick fur as I stroke out into the pond.

The crystal clear waters flow around slowly, bioluminescent rays of sunlight being cast about, caustic patterns drawn along the bottom with a hypnotizing dance.

I swim out farther, catching up to Waya's floating image in the watery depths, and surface for air.

"Oh! Hi. Enjoying the swim?"

"Yeah, it's great out here."

"And totally private." She paddles around in a lazy circle. "Nobody's ever bothered me out here, so it's excellent for some peace and quiet."

I half-heartedly imitate her circling pattern, our movements casting soft swirls around us.

Waya splashes water at me without warning. "Stop following me."

I reciprocate her kindness, a small wave washing over her face as she tries to block it, doing little to protect her. "Then stop going in circles."

Laughter emanates from the both of us as we try to best each other, exhaustion soon taking over from our arms swinging recklessly.

Kicking our legs, I follow her over to the base of the waterfall, large rocks jutting out from beneath. Waya sits on one as I remain floating in the water, watching her enjoy a fine mist from the cascade.

She reclines, looking down at me. "Oh c'mon, you saw that hardly any of my old pack wore clothes. Live a little."

I climb onto the rock. Sitting beside her, my head gets a little extra shower from a wayward fall. Waya giggles and slides a few inches over, and I nudge myself closer, shaking my head to clear off some of the water.

The rushing noise of the falls combined with scintillating waters both energizes and calms me, my mind spacing out as I breathe heavily, sighing away any worry of the world.

"Beautiful, isn't it?" Waya leans forward, admiring the same scene with a smile. "Some of the others have come here with me on a few occasions, but I don't think anyone enjoyed it as much as I have. Eventually, it just became my place to get away."

"I can see the appeal." I fidget, scratching at the stone with a claw. "Waya, why do some wolves go berserk? From what you say, even the most experienced werewolves can be triggered by something, and in my case, it only happened when I was heavily provoked, despite how new I am."

She takes her time before answering, visible thinking traced on her face. "Your wolf was just as scared as you. He might have all the senses of nature, but he's never been exposed to the dangers of the outside world, if that makes sense. Sometimes that fear can manifest in a malicious way. Also, you hadn't been given the time to properly bond.

"As for others, aside from how you treat your wolf, it all comes down to your own nature as well. Some people can be extra careless, or even mean to begin with. A wolf might clash with that person's abused traits."

"But isn't your wolf inherently part of you?"

Waya frowns. "There's one more factor that most don't talk about…" Another moment passes as she considers how to tell me, if at all.

I stop scratching and rest my hand upon her shoulder. "No matter what it is, I won't judge you for telling me."

She closes her eyes, speaking with hesitation. "… My own wolf's DNA is a part of you, along with fragments of memories and experiences. Precursory wolf experiences don't get passed down, as far as I know." Waya stares hard at me before continuing. "But that's why we don't try to bite other humans. That's why I called it a curse. You're going to suffer mentally because of what I went through, Leon, and the more you get to know me, the more those fragments are going to surface."

I hold her gaze, rejecting the thought of severing my friendship. "I'm not afraid."

"But I'm afraid for *you!*" Her head leans on my hand, a couple of tears trickling between my fingers. "You don't deserve to deal with the pain I went through."

"Maybe not, but that's hardly something I can let stand in the way of our friendship."

"You're too kind, Leon. Please don't let that be your downfall."

Shifted out and clothed, we wander back to our current site. The evening sun is against our backs, long shadows leading the way across barren ground.

"Thanks for going swimming with me. It was a lot of fun."

"We ought to go again some time when it gets warmer. If you want to, that is."

"I'd love to."

"By the way, I'm sorry for bringing up more questions about our wolves."

"No, it's okay. You should know about these things. Nobody told me about that other stuff until my wolf began to freak out in situations that weren't even a threat to me. It took a couple of months to happen, but as it started, that's when Locan explained everything. If anything, I could've told you sooner."

With only two nights before our full shift, I feel that it's best to try and learn all I can. If anybody can prepare me for that time, it's Waya.

Chapter 14

The next day brings an unpleasant drift with it, snow resting upon much of my body as I wake to a bright, afternoon sun peeking out from a cloudy sky. The mockery of the star does nothing to help me warm up as I shake the flakes from my coat, breathing out in a frigid atmosphere. I think of shifting to bulk up for extra warmth, but decide for Waya to return.

She apparently went out before I got up, probably for a morning hunt or something. I'm sure I could handle my wolf with no problems, but I still feel better knowing she's around if something were to happen.

Gathering some loose sticks and branches, I take to making a fire, only to realize I never went back for the tools.

I drop the bundle of wood with a sigh, Waya returning just as I do so.

"Leon, what are you doing? Building a stick fort?" She smiles, handing me a mole. "It isn't much, but it's the least I could do."

"Thank you. And I was going to, but then I noticed that there wasn't enough to make you a master bedroom of your own, so I gave up."

With a roll of her eyes, she begins to eat.

"I was just thinking about how useful it would be about now to have that tool bag I picked up."

Waya swallows. "Oh. Well, you've been getting along just fine without it."

"I know, but it wouldn't hurt to make an easy fire now and then to stay warm."

"My own fur's been pretty sufficient for a long time. I know yours is still growing in when you're out of form, but you can always shift when you need to."

"That's true. It'd also be nice to pick up some extra food here and there. You know, like you did when you came into town."

She lowers her hands, half-eaten squirrel dangling by the tail. "Fine... whatever. We'll go back tomorrow."

I'm slightly unnerved by Waya's response. Even though it seems to upset her, I can't help but to feel out of place being so far from the town. Being back around there should help us stay fed well.

At the same time, being out in the wilderness seems strangely familiar, but that could also be her wolf's memories. Being able to survive as much as we have on our own impresses me, even if it's only been a little over a week separated from her pack. She relied upon the others, and I relied on the settlement providing my needs.

Am I really going to stoop back down for help from humans?

My head shakes at the thought. *What? But... I am human.*

You betray us.

I'm doing what's good for us both!

A heavy sigh escapes me, and I find it weird to argue with myself, or rather, with my own wolf. Maybe we're just hungry.

***

I wake, senses overwhelmed with a powerful drive. Shifting immediately, I strain to track the direction of my prey, ready to kill.

As soon as I'm finished, I leap into action, running at full speed to catch up before it's too late.

Rounding a few trees, the animal notices my approach and speeds off, only making me hungrier. There's no way I'm gonna lose this time.

My sight is out of focus, likely due to being so esurient. *I need to feed! Now!*

I kick up the ground, ripping through the woods at maddening pace. Hard as I try, a tree seems to get in my way every time I'm mere inches from pouncing. With one last thrust of energy, I break the barrier and tackle my prey, staring it down before I deliver the killing blow.

Waya's eyes stare back at me, icy with fear, but I ignore her and drive my fangs deep, wiping out the life from her gaze.

I feel a nudge in my side, waking me from a deep sleep. Sweat runs between my underfur, chilling from the air as it circulates.

"Getting up? We're going back, aren't we?"

It's already mid-afternoon. I don't remember doing much of anything yesterday after our discussion of returning to the outer town. I try to push the nightmare from my mind.

Waya seems anxious, lumbering back and forth in her wolf form. She's mumbling to herself.

I start to shift, thinking my wolf would be excited to go for a run today as we make our way back toward the town. I'm gonna have to treat him to a nice steak when we return.

"It's about time, Leon. Gosh, it's like you sleep a full day's worth away every other day." Waya bats at a stick as I watch it fly several yards. "You can be lazy when I do the shopping."

"I'm going to help, Waya. It's not like I'll sleep and eat while you go begging."

"Just hurry up."

The same irritability is presented as was before the coyote attack. This time, I'm determined to keep her in my sights. This female doesn't need to cause any more trouble for me...

When I'm done, we both head out, kicking up frozen leaves as we race through the deadened forest together. With each breath, I feel more and more awake, happy for a change of pace. It's been a bit boring out here, but this adventure ought to bring some new challenges, and I'm ready for it.

I see Waya bound over a fallen tree in my peripheral vision, seamlessly keeping her pace as she lands. Coming up on a boulder, I try the same, almost slipping on some underbrush when I come down.

She huffs while we continue to run. "Trying to impress me? How about you just try to keep up instead." Waya starts to pick up speed, getting ahead of me by a few yards.

One by one, the obstacles pass by as we jump, round, crouch, and climb our way through the woods, her chosen path giving me plenty of exercise and practice.

My chest tightens as we press onward. "Waya, slow down a bit. I might not be able to match your pace forever."

"Nuh-uh. You wanna get better? Then do it!" Tirelessly, she makes an insane jump across a wide gully, easing her drop with the grab of a branch.

Following through with the same jump, I second-guess myself at the last moment. I try to grab a wayward tree limb halfway over the gap, but it snaps, dropping me into the brush.

Waya laughs hysterically. "Nice landing! You should've seen your face on the way down."

I crawl my way up and out of the gully, staring her down. "How about a bit of physical training instead?"

Before she can react, I leap at Waya, knocking her to the ground. We try to wrestle each other down, keen to get the upper hand on one another.

"You think you can best me, Leon? I'm way above your league!"

"I might not have experience like you, but I can hold my own!" I pin her down.

"That much is true, but you're still learning." She shoves her feet against me, launching me as her body rolls over into a side leap, forcing me down hard.

Totally winded, I feebly grab at her arms, unable to move beneath her weight. "Okay, you win."

"Speak up. I can't hear you."

I exert a forceful gasp. "Can I breathe now?"

Waya smiles, letting me up. "Of course!" She sits, watching me find my footing as I stand. "But, as the loser, you have to find us something to eat."

"Since when did we decide that?"

"Just now."

I sigh. "Fine, but I get the first few bites."

"Fine." She smirks. "Now go."

Chapter 15

A red-orange sun slowly descends toward the horizon, hazy shadows reaching across the bleak landscape. A soft but chilly breeze pushes a few loose leaves around.

We're unshifted, enjoying my kill of deer.

"It's an excellent meal after such a long run back."

"Thanks, Waya. He was pretty easy to get." I finish off the marrow from a bone and grab another, looking up at the sky as I mull the day over. "Tonight's the night, isn't it?"

"Yeah, the first of three."

"Is there anything else I should know?"

She grabs the last leg from the deer, thoughtful consideration in her eyes. "Just try not to let your wolf's thoughts cloud your judgment too much. This will be his first time actually getting to lead, and you're gonna have to really work for taking action. A full shift should never be taken lightly, and he'll still need your help learning what not to do."

"Will your wolf have trouble with him as far as dominance goes?"

"No. I'll make sure she gets the picture and keep her submissive. I apologize in advance if she makes a better suggestion in a situation."

"So, three days and nights of nothing but wolf, right? And there's no way to shift out?"

"Not at all. Most of my old pack's tried that many times, but nobody ever succeeded. If anything, the wolf just gets angry that you're trying to dismiss it." Waya gives a short giggle, then goes somber. "Your dreams will also be affected harshly, if that hasn't happened already."

"I told you, Waya, I'm not afraid."

"I know… but it's still a lot to handle. Don't lie to me and tell me that it hasn't made you more wary."

She's right. With many of my actions, I'm beginning to second-guess myself, sometimes unsure of how to proceed. Even when I don't think about it, I can still feel my indecisiveness. We don't need me getting us into unnecessary trouble.

Her arms cross. "Not admitting that won't make it easier to cope with."

I sigh, thinking about the images that flash into my mind. "The nightmares aren't pleasant, but I promise I'm doing what I can to focus on what matters."

"Dang it, Leon." She claws at a tree. "I'm not worth the trouble. Why can't you get that?"

"You're not trouble. I thought we got through that already. I'm not a fair-weather friend. And besides, I know I can't do this alone."

"Figures. I honestly shouldn't be surprised, but you're hard to understand sometimes."

"Being misunderstood seems to be a recurring thing with me."

Waya lightly punches my shoulder. "C'mon, let's get there before dark."

We pick up the trail again, sated from a hearty meal, our wolves content and happy with us. There's only a couple of miles to go, and walking gives us a chance to recuperate for night.

Skies grow ever darker as we near the outskirts of the town, familiar woods catching my senses. In addition to my wolf recognizing the land, I see my old cave, the fortification hardly touched, save for some graffiti and a couple of beer bottles. The bag of tools I had borrowed seems to be gone.

"Home sweet home, huh?" Waya says as she inspects the damage. "These locals get more and more creative."

"It's almost weird to be back here."

"I'm willing to bet that your wolf wishes he were back in the deep forest now."

I smile. "Once again, you know what he's thinking."

"He makes it easy to know his thoughts when we're shifted. Body language is very expressive, and I could see his gradual discomfort while we were headed back here."

With a sniff, I kick at one of the bottles. "He doesn't want to be here, but he's too lazy to run back right now."

She chortles. "Tell him that he's going to be doing all the work for three days. Maybe he'll actually let you take the reins."

I kneel instantly, almost doubled over in a wave of pain.

"Leon, what's wrong?!"

"I… think it's… happening."

"Hey, you're gonna be just fine. It'll be a bit for me since—"

Waya's words are drowned out as my ears ring, my clawed hands grasping my head as I lay against the ground. Her mouth moves, but I can't make sense of what I hear. My body is rigid and partially numb, but I can still feel pain coursing through me as I shift out of control.

While my wolf continues to surface, Waya kneels by my side, never taking focus away from me.

As to why she's grabbing my arms, I don't know, but she needs to back off so I can breathe.

"Leon, I'm trying to help you. Don't do this to me."

I back up hastily, terrified of this creature. "Who are you? Where is she?"

She stares into my eyes, a hard leer confusing me. "So be it..." The creature assumes a seemingly submissive position, her stance practiced. I'm not sure what's going on, but I take a few more steps back, both in awe and scared. I want to run away, but my limbs don't respond.

Why can't I move? What's going on?

Her own cries disrupt me, and I toss my head trying to clear the sound. A moment later, I see her, the one I know.

I lope over to her, hoping she recognizes me.

"Told you I wouldn't leave you alone," she says.

"You weren't here. Where did you go?"

"The others needed me, but I'm here now."

"Are we hunting?"

"No, we're just scouting the area. Let's take a look around."

The female leads me around, familiarizing herself with my territory as we ensure that no trespassers are present.

Her name is Waya...

What is Waya?

"Waya?"

"Yeah, Leon?"

I shake my head. "Sorry, I'm just confused."

"It's okay. That's going to happen a lot for a couple of nights while you and your wolf adjust more to one another."

As the night goes by, we traverse the woods with hunger, our wolves needing serious sustenance after the long journey back. Every few hours, any food I've eaten seems to not matter as much as it would have only a month ago. I thought my metabolism kept me consistently hungry enough before, but now it's almost become voracious with the fuller moon.

We each find a small but decent kill and, not long after, find sleep.

Chapter 16

The next evening, a harsh breeze chills the forest, and I'm grateful to have no choice but to be shifted. Any trace of human features has all but left me a few nights ago, and I can imagine how I'll look when the full shift is over.

We're lumbering along aimlessly, tracking for any peculiar scents. Since it's been a little while, there may be a pitched tent or something around, which would explain the vandalism this far out.

"Do you think we'll find any ruffians, Waya?"

"I'm not sure, but I don't like that scent I'm picking up."

Not a moment after she says something do I notice it. More pungent with each step, there's an array of scents that unsettle me. Beer, sweat, and… gunpowder, acrid on the wind.

Curiosity gets the better of us and we edge closer to inaudible banter.

"… without any viable proof."

"I'm telling you what I saw! If you're too stupid to believe me, then that's on you guys."

I stop dead in my tracks, afraid to even turn my neck to look over at Waya.

A light whisper escapes her mouth. "Leon, that isn't... is it?"

"It is."

Run!

Run?

Run, now!

I quickly take off in the opposite direction, feeling extreme anxiety for a situation I've yet to perceive. Hearing the sound of my old girlfriend's voice out here in the woods sends an inexplicable horror through my mind.

Waya doesn't dare speak as she runs after me, her distinct steps urging me faster.

Suddenly, a gunshot goes off, followed by a few voices.

"Did you see that?"

"I almost hit it. Call it in!"

A shrill screech pierces the cold, night air. "I told you! Kill it, now!"

"Hey, it's me. We just saw it again, out back of..."

We run as fast as we ever have, desperation to escape a coming demise on our heels.

About six minutes later, we hear sirens of an approaching squad and the shouting of the individuals we briefly heard before running.

"Leon, are you okay?"

I hardly notice her speaking, the trees whipping passed me at an alarming speed.

"Leon!"

My feet skid, almost tripping me as I stop. "What?"

"Don't stop, you idiot!"

We start running again. "Sorry, my wolf is scared."

"And you? You're going in random directions!"

"Yeah… I'm scared too. What do you expect?!"

"Hey, don't take it out on me! Sorry you couldn't keep that girl on a leash, but now's *not* the time to lose your cool!"

Running for our lives, the sound of bullets rip through the air within mere inches from us, soon joined by more guns.

"Waya, where can we hide?" I run alongside her, panting heavily from exerting myself.

"Quick, go through the draw! Everyone should have a hard time following us there."

We make our way into the depths, steep hills running upward from either side of us. A few of our pursuers trail us, but eventually decide to hold back, taking random shots at us from the far end of the valley.

Slowing down, I take a glance behind us. "Do you think we're safe now?"

"Not sure." Waya stops, sitting between a couple of leaning trees nearby to catch her breath. "Hopefully those guys get the idea and… leave us alone."

I lay against one of the ridges near a boulder. "I'm sorry for bringing this upon us."

"It's not your fault, Leon. You were only—"

A bullet hits the dirt, a sudden visible gash across Waya's scapula.

"Waya! Are you alright?"

"Yeah… I'll be fine. It just stings." She's bracing her shoulder with a wince, then looks up in horror. "Oh my gosh. We're being flanked from uphill!"

As Waya crouches beside a larger tree, I sit behind her, taking a closer look. "It's not too bad."

"Don't even think about cleaning it right now. We're in *way* too dangerous of a spot."

I withdraw my tongue, unwilling to admit anything.

The men start shouting, faint outlines of bodies slowly descending from tree to tree, the angle of the slopes threatening a quick descent. Flashlights scan the floor of the draw, beams getting closer by the second. Feeling intense pressure from the beleaguered circumstance, I pace frantically.

"I'm scared, Waya. I… need to run!"

"Leon, don't! Don't give in to your wolf now!"

Struggling to keep him under control, I clasp my head in hand, straining to shut out the occasional gunshot between the yelling.

Run! Run, now!

As I consider taking off, a harsh pain strikes the side of my left thigh, searing heat drilled deep into my leg. "Aargh!"

Waya rests her free arm on my leg. "I'm sorry. We should've run sooner than later." She punches the ground. "I can't believe we're going to die like prey!"

Heavy footsteps close in, no more than a few yards away from us, before a shrill howl pierces the night air. Our ears perk up to several more howls from the east, answering the call.

"Leon… that's…!"

Between my own breathing and stifled hearing, I notice a new voice shouting above the rest. "Tano, take Manita and Intama with you up the north side! Kiramu, go with Lena and Tilan along the south! Kemalu, you, Mituna and Kenami stay back and watch for an opening."

My eyes watch as each wolf goes to the designated locations, synced flawlessly as a whole. Before any guns can effectively turn toward the approaching assistance, several shouts of pain and fear reverberate throughout the trees, the draw falling dark once again as our assailants begin to flee.

Locan ambles over. "Ah, you're not dead. Good, then you two can follow me as we drive these monsters out of here."

"We can't, Locan. Leon's hurt."

He observes my leg, then looks back to Waya. "Let him stay here. Come with me, Waya."

"We're not abandoning him!"

Locan huffs, clearly irritated. "I'm not suggesting that. He'll obviously slow us down, so we'll come back for him."

"Oh." She gets up from the ground, looking to me briefly. "I promise I'll be back."

The two run to join the rest of her pack, my senses barely able to hang on. Then, all goes black.

I feel my leg being propped up, thigh sore from resting at an angle.

"How bad is it?"

My eye squints, and I see Locan standing off to the side, a couple of his pack nearby.

"Pretty bad." Waya gently parts the fur on my leg as she inspects the wound. "It's deep, and it's not going to heal like this."

Both my eyes open as I raise my head to see what she's doing. "Waya?"

"You got shot. The bullet didn't pass through."

"... What are you suggesting?"

I hear Locan sigh. "Kemalu, Tano, hold him steady."

As the two wolves firmly grasp my arms and legs, Waya frowns, her eyes glossing over. "Leon... this is going to hurt..." She extends a claw and looks down, focused intently.

My teeth grit hard, and I'm unable to bite back a scream, silence of the forest amplifying a roar of sheer agony.

A full minute of indescribable torture later and I'm panting heavily, on the verge of passing out again.

Waya examines the object. "Huh, I'm surprised it was a nine-millimeter. Thank God it wasn't a hollow point."

Chapter 17

Our would-be killers were successfully scattered from the forest, the din of death's shadow echoing in my mind as my heart slows. Not even a month into the new year, and I feel we've got our fill of crazed action for the months ahead.

Waya's pack begins to assemble, random soft chatter making its way amongst everyone.

Locan, Tano, Kemalu and Waya return to me, Manita tagging along from a small distance. From the sound in Locan's voice, it seems the pack did a better job than expected.

"I'm proud of this pack, and glad you're all more controlled than we were five years ago. Hopefully none of those men contracted, but if so, then it isn't our problem."

Kemalu speaks. "Too bad we couldn't get Tilan to stop chasing after a couple of the tougher guys deeper into the woods. He probably won't be back until sunrise."

"Still sitting like maimed prey?" Tano says, scoffing at my injured state. "You should clean that wound already."

I furrow my brows. "I would, if I could *reach.*"

Manita perks up. "Maybe I could help you with that."

"No!"

Waya's sudden outburst causes the whole pack to fall silent, a heavy fluster edging in on her face. "Um, no, I… I can help him, Manita."

I catch the hint of a snide smirk gracing Locan's face. "Let's go, everyone. We have a late meal to catch." He starts to leave, the rest of the wolves gathering around him, and then rounds to glance at us with a decisive glare. "Waya, we'll be a few miles east. Leon… welcome to the pack." Within seconds, everyone is gone.

A smile crosses Waya. "Leon, Locan accepted you." She hugs me, then retracts. "Sorry. It's just… he never accepts anyone on a whim like that, especially after the way he treated you the first time."

"I'm glad. Honestly, I thought I'd wind up as food by the end of all this."

She leans down to examine my leg again, brushing the fur clean of leaf and twig.

"By the way, uh, thanks for… for helping."

Waya leers at me with a humorless look. "Don't be weird about it."

Morning dawns, my mind swimming from the events of last night. I was unable to sleep much, but my wolf doesn't appear to be phased. If anything, he's just hungry.

It's the final day of our full shift, and all I want to do is go for a run. To get far away from here and never return.

Waya takes her time getting up, clearly exhausted. She glances around languidly, as if she's trying to gauge our situation.

"Hey, Waya. You okay?"

"Yeah, I'm fine." She nods with a yawn. "How's your leg?"

"Much better. It's still a little sore, but I think a good run will take care of that."

A short huff of amusement comes from her. "I'm ready to go when you are."

Despite the fact that the sun has barely begun to rise, both my wolf and I are raring to rush the day headlong. After the insanity we went through together, I don't care what anyone throws at us.

By the time we get moving for the day, I realize that Waya is following me, letting me lead the run.

She notices my glance as we're running. "It's okay, Leon. I trust that your wolf knows what he's doing. Go wherever he takes you."

So we run. For hours, we wander all around the woods, a brisk day holding nothing more for us than the sheer thrill of enjoying a good adventure to nowhere in particular.

For the first time in my life, I feel truly free. Not just from the general fatigue of contemporary living standards, but in my ability to see the world in a new light. Even when I have no destination in mind, it's like I know where to go, and how to get there.

As my wolf takes me along, I allow my own mind to settle, almost as if I'm seeing through the eyes of someone else. Once again, I'm taken back to the past, as I had felt myself dreaming that lonely night, when in reality I was experiencing my first hunt. Floating, flying through the trees without a care in the world, content on finding food and solace in the unknown.

I will never go back, and I'll never have to.

Eventually, we make our way out where we once were before, toward the deep and distant woodland heart of being who we are. The main territory of Waya's pack, and my new home.

The trek took all day, our mindless wandering carrying us into the dusk.

"So, we're finally back." Waya presses her hands against the dirt, claws kneading the ground as she breathes the air heavily.

I nod. "And as far as I'm concerned, here to stay."

She smiles. "I couldn't be happier to be out here. There's no room for beings like us in society. Begging for scraps and loose change wasn't my idea of a good time, and I'd rather be hunting for my own food anyway." Waya looks down. "Speaking of which, I'm up for a bite after running all day."

"Let's hunt, then." I flex my shoulders and hands, a grin emerging at the thought of fresh prey.

A short excursion brings us upon the trail of a hearty scent, tracks in a light layer of snow patches becoming more evident.

The moose's tracks don't lead far from us, as we soon find our target traipsing along. He's completely unaware of our presence.

Without notice, I dash in, pouncing upon him with ferocity, keen to taste fresh blood. He almost buckles at the combination of both surprise and weight. I grip on, claws extended to the fullest. His head swings wildly, antlers striking me in the face, and I slip off, my focus disoriented for a moment.

Before the moose can escape, Waya rounds the front, slashing at his legs. As she halts his movement, I regain my stance and leap again. Our efforts are in perfect sync, taking down the prey with ease.

I deliver the final blow, teeth driven deeply.

Panting heavily, I sit in contemplation, grateful for the provision we happened across. It ought to sate us for a solid day.

Waya sits opposite of me as she cleans her paws. Our kill is settled between, heat emanating of a job well done escaping from his body.

"We make a pretty great team, Leon. I'm glad to know another wolf that can work so well with me. You certainly earn your keep."

With a nod, I go to feed, hesitating for only a second, then looking back up at her. "Waya..." I resettle my feet. "... Will you share this kill with me?"

A surprised look crosses her face, before being replaced with a felicitous glance in surety as she stares into my eyes. "Yes."

Unfortunately, wolves have been largely
extirpated from Maine by the end of the
nineteenth century. Even still, the state
may see an occasional wolf from Canada.
It is of my personal hope that, someday,
wolves may be reintroduced to the natural
habitats available in Maine.

Raise notice on behalf of these beautiful
creatures via Wolf Awareness Week! 🐾

www.ingramcontent.com/pod-product-compliance
Lightning Source LLC
Chambersburg PA
CBHW010348220726
48290CB00016B/2677